PUFFIN BOOKS

UK | USA | Canada | Ireland | Australia
India | New Zealand | South Africa

Puffin Books is part of the Penguin Random House group of companies
whose addresses can be found at global.penguinrandomhouse.com.

www.penguin.co.uk
www.puffin.co.uk
www.ladybird.co.uk

Penguin
Random House
UK

First published 2017
001

Written by Rebecca Lewis-Oakes
With thanks to Liss Norton
Illustrated by Helen Sinclair
Cover illustration by Faye Yong
Text and illustrations copyright © Arklu Limited, 2017
© 2012 Arklu Limited. Lottie is a trademark of Arklu Limited.

Printed in Great Britain by Clays Ltd, St Ives plc

A CIP catalogue record for this book is available from the British Library

ISBN: 978–1–409–39311–5

All correspondence to:
Puffin Books
Penguin Random House Children's
80 Strand, London WC2R 0RL

Lottie

Lottie Solves a Mystery

LUCIE BRAVEHEART

PUFFIN

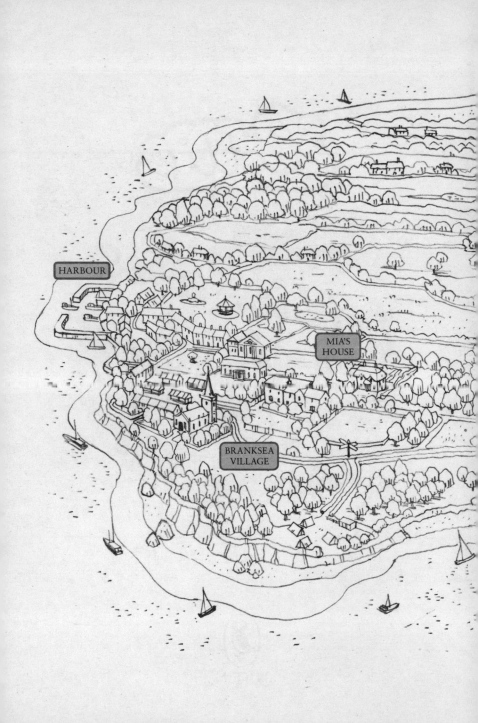

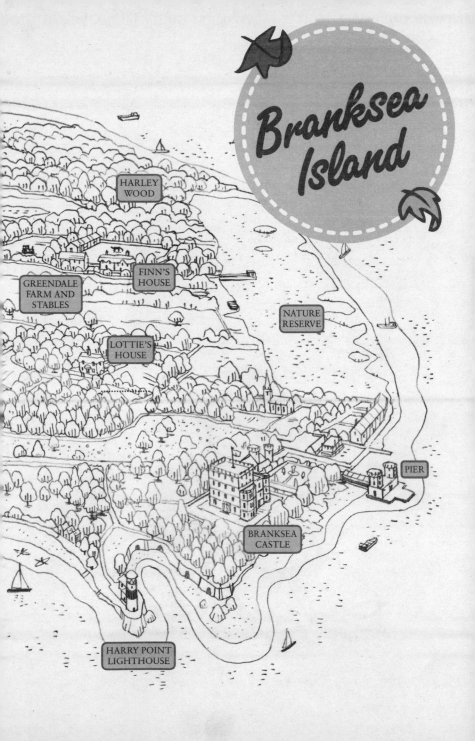

Contents

Chapter One
Treasure in the Attic

'Ladies and gentlemen! Say hello to Biscuit, the amazing, the incredible . . . wonder dog!' In the middle of the living room, Lottie spread her arms out wide as if she was a performer on stage.

Biscuit, her beagle puppy, wagged his tail.

Lottie let her arms fall to her sides and sighed. 'Come on, Biscuit. Try it! Stand on two legs.'

Biscuit sat down on the rug.

'I'll show you,' said Lottie. She rubbed her hands together, then flipped up into a handstand.

Biscuit trotted over and licked her nose.

Lottie fell in a heap, giggling. 'Silly Biscuit,' she said, giving him a hug.

'What was that crash?' Mum called from upstairs.

'Nothing, Mum!' said Lottie. 'I was just trying to train Biscuit to be a circus dog.'

'Well, why don't you both come and help me clear out the attic instead?' Mum replied.

Lottie looked out of the window. It was still raining. She had wanted to take Biscuit for a lovely, muddy morning walk, but clearing the attic could be fun, too. There might be treasure up there!

'Come on, Biscuit. Let's see if

you can be an amazing, incredible treasure-hunting dog!'

Lottie and Biscuit bounded up the stairs.

The attic had a sloping ceiling and a round window at one end. It also had lots of cobwebs, dust and boxes.

'I'm looking for something we can take to the charity jumble sale,' said Mum.

Biscuit barked beside the first pile of boxes, which contained a tree, tinsel and lots of fairy lights.

'No, Biscuit,' said Lottie.
'Those are our Christmas
decorations. We need those!
What else can you find?'
Suddenly Biscuit sneezed.

'What is it, Biscuit?' asked Lottie. She went over to her puppy as he began to tug at a dusty blanket. 'Let me help.'

Lottie pulled the blanket off. 'Wow!'

Underneath was the most amazing suitcase. It was very old, and made of worn brown leather with metal corners. There were faded labels all over it with the names of faraway places like Nigeria, Nepal and Canada.

Lottie carefully clicked the locks. The suitcase creaked open. Inside were all kinds of strange and beautiful things. A red dress with gold stitching and sparkling buttons lay on top.

'That's Great-aunt Matilda's

Chinese dress!' said Mum.
'You've found her suitcase.'
'Wow! Do I have a Chinese
great-aunt?' asked Lottie.

'Well, actually she's your great-great-aunt. I used to call her Gam – G-A-M, for Great-aunt Matilda! She wasn't Chinese, but she did travel to China,' said Mum. 'She was a brave adventurer. She went all over the world and kept the special things she found on her travels in this suitcase.'

'Can I look through it?' asked Lottie.

'Yes, if you're careful. Some of those things will be over

a hundred years old.' Mum
smiled.

Lottie gave Biscuit a big
cuddle. 'You really are an
amazing, incredible
treasure-hunting dog!'

Chapter Two
A Totally Amazing Idea!

There were all kinds of treasures in Gam's suitcase. Lottie found a pile of hats, a scarf covered in stars, and a huge shell. When Lottie held the shell up to her ear, she could hear the sound of the sea.

Biscuit yipped and pushed a cowboy hat towards Lottie.

There was a battered red
leather notebook underneath.
As Lottie picked it up, a black-
and-white photo fell out.

It showed a woman with a big smile standing in front of some elephants. She was wearing sturdy boots, an old-fashioned sun hat and –

'The starry scarf!' cried Lottie. 'This must be Great-aunt Matilda!'

Lottie couldn't wait to find out more about Gam. She opened the notebook. The first page was titled 'Beasts of the World'. Flipping through the book, Lottie could see that

Gam had travelled to all sorts of countries. This first section of the notebook was all about her time as an explorer, searching for legendary beasts in every corner of the world!

There was an entry about a huge, apelike creature called Bigfoot from the forests of the Rocky Mountains, with a drawing of a giant footprint alongside. There were pictures of lake monsters from Spain and Sweden. And Lottie could

hardly believe the entry on the
Bunyip from Australia – Gam
had written 'Watch out for the
teeth!' next to an animal that
was half crocodile, half bird!

Lottie wished she could be
an adventurer. There were so
many exciting things to
discover in the world!

She returned to the front of
the notebook. On the second
page was a list called 'Rules
for Good Beast-hunting'.
Rule Number One said:

'Record evidence of strange and mysterious events.'

Suddenly Lottie had a totally amazing idea. If Gam had gone on beast hunts, why couldn't Lottie go on one now, right here on Branksea Island?

'Mum, please can I call Mia and Finn?' asked Lottie. 'I've got an idea!'

Mum dusted off her jeans and smiled. 'Of course. Let's invite them for lunch.'

Mia arrived first on her bike.
She was wearing a red
mackintosh, wellies and her dad's
fishing hat because of the rain.

Lottie gave Mia a big hug and laughed as her friend shook the rain out of her curly hair. Mia quickly checked her cochlear implant – it was still dry.

Then Finn whizzed up on his scooter and gave them both high fives.

Lottie and Mia could tell that he had come across the fields of his family's farm – his scooter was even more mucky than usual!

Mia and Finn said hello to Lottie's mum, then helped themselves to sandwiches. They headed up to Lottie's bedroom with their lunch.

'So, what's up?' asked Finn, as the three friends settled down on Lottie's bed.

Lottie showed them Gam's notebook.

'I found this in the attic,' she
said. 'My great-great-aunt was
a brave adventurer! She wrote
about all these amazing beasts.

31

And she tried to track them down in Australia and Canada and Sweden and Spain! So –' Lottie took a deep breath – 'we should go on a beast hunt, too!'

'Where?' asked Mia.

'Right here on Branksea Island,' said Lottie. 'Gam found legendary beasts all over the world. Why wouldn't there be some here, too?'

'My dad thinks there's a beast in Harley Wood,' said Finn through a mouthful of sandwich.

'He's heard strange noises
coming from there, and some
of our farm fences have been
knocked down.'

'See? We've found a clue already!' cried Lottie. 'This can be our very first adventure!'

Chapter Three
Gathering Evidence

The next day the rain cleared and it was bright and sunny. Mia and Finn met Lottie and Biscuit at Harley Wood. Lottie brought Gam's notebook, and Mia had her camera to record evidence.

'Gam says you should start a beast hunt by looking for

some tracks,' said Lottie.

The three friends walked into the wood. After a while, they passed little red-and-white toadstools, and the wood grew damper and darker.

'It's a bit spooky in here,' said

Mia. 'Could the beast be hiding
in the shadows?'

Finn shivered. 'What if the
beast is following *us*?'

Suddenly Biscuit growled.
The fur on his neck stood on
end and he pulled at his lead.

'What did you see, Biscuit?' asked Lottie.

The puppy was pulling so hard at his lead that he yanked Lottie forward. She tried to keep up, but the lead slipped out of her hand.

'Biscuit!' Lottie shouted. 'Come back!'

But the little dog charged off into the wood. The three friends ran after Biscuit, calling his name. They jumped over thick tree roots and ducked under low-hanging branches.

Lottie's heart was pounding. What if her puppy got lost in the big wood? What if the beast found him before they did?

Then she heard a familiar whimpering sound. Biscuit! His lead was caught on a tree root.

'There you are!' Lottie gave him a big cuddle and untangled his lead. 'You mustn't run off, Biscuit,' she said in a firm voice.

Biscuit licked her face, as if to say sorry.

'Why did you run away, Biscuit?' asked Mia. 'Did you see something?'

Lottie looked around. 'I can't see any tracks,' she said. 'Maybe he smelled something. Dogs have a much better sense of smell than humans do.'

'What if he sniffed out the beast?' asked Mia, her eyes wide.

'Guys, I've found something!' called Finn.

Lottie and Mia couldn't see him any more, but Biscuit sniffed and pulled at his lead. He knew the way.

Finn was standing next to a tall beech tree.

'*Ta-da!*' he said, pointing to deep scratch marks in the bark.

'That is definitely evidence of a beast!' said Lottie.

Mia took a few photos, then looked at the marks more closely. 'The marks are quite deep,' she said. 'So the beast must be pretty strong.'

'And it must have sharp claws,' said Finn.

Just then Lottie spotted a tuft

of black fur caught on a low
branch. 'I bet this came from
our beast, too,' she said.

Mia took a photo of the fur,
and Lottie tucked it into the
notebook as evidence.

'We know a lot about the beast already. It has black fur and strong claws,' said Lottie.

'And we know it's nearby,' said Mia, looking around nervously.

'Ruff!' barked Biscuit, and the friends all jumped. Then they laughed.

Finn shook his head. 'I didn't really believe we would find the beast that knocked down my dad's fence. But now I'm not so sure . . .'

Chapter Four
A Beastly Photo

'We need more evidence of this beast,' said Lottie.

Mia held out her camera. 'How about we set up a camera trap?' she suggested. 'I could leave my camera here on a timer to take photos every ten minutes. If the beast comes back, we'll get a picture of it!'

Mia tucked the camera under
a tree root, where it wouldn't
get wet if it rained. If the beast
came back to this spot, then

hopefully Mia's camera would snap a photo of it!

'Let's come back after school tomorrow to check it,' said Finn.

'Ruff!' Biscuit barked in agreement, and the friends set off for home.

Lottie was so excited about the pictures they might find on Mia's camera that she could hardly sleep that night. She took out Gam's notebook as bedtime reading.

MOKÈLÉ-MBÈMBÉ
CONGO RIVER

REPORTED SIGHTING: 'swimming dinosaur' living in river.

EVIDENCE: sunset, riverbanks: big-cat paw prints, ribbon-like snake prints. No Mokèlé-mbèmbé tracks. Dawn, further upriver: huge footprints with webbed toes!

NOTE TO SELF: don't run along muddy banks. You will fall in and get told off by your guide! (Guide not very excited about Mokèlé-mbèmbé.)

CONCLUSION: footprints may
be evidence of Mokèlé-mbèmbé.
Unfortunately, had to leave before
further sightings.

Lottie giggled. Gam was so
brave. Lottie was determined to
be just as fearless in her search
for the beast of Branksea.

After school the next day
Lottie, Finn and Mia raced to
the woods as soon as they could.
Mia's older brother, Sammi,

was with them – they had all
stayed late for drama club.

'How long are you guys
going to be?' asked Sammi,

kicking at some leaves. 'I want to go home and watch TV.'

'Don't be grumpy, Sammi,' said Mia. 'Let's see what's on my camera!'

The friends all huddled round Mia's camera.

'Trees, trees, trees,' said Finn, as Mia flicked through the photos.

'Trees, trees – oh!' said Lottie. Two big eyes were staring back at them from the camera screen.

'We've got it! This must be the beast of Branksea!' Mia whooped.

'The *what* of Branksea?' asked Sammi.

'The beast,' said Lottie
excitedly. 'We found its claw
marks and fur, and now we have
a picture of it. Well, of its eyes.'

Sammi took the camera from
Mia. 'That could be anything,'
he said. 'It's so close to the

camera you can't tell what it is.'

Lottie sighed. Sammi was taking all the fun out of their beast hunt.

Finn heard Lottie sigh and jumped in a muddy puddle to make the others laugh.

'That's it!' said Lottie. 'We can set a muddy trap for the beast's footprint.' *Just like Gam did with Mokèlé-mbèmbé!* she thought.

Lottie got her water bottle out of her bag and poured the water over the ground near the tree to make a muddy puddle.

'Let's come back tomorrow and see what we find!' she said.

Chapter Five
Night Prowler

'Do you think we'll find any tracks in the wood tonight?' asked Finn, as the three friends ate their school lunches.

'I hope so!' said Lottie.

Mia sighed. 'Sammi doesn't think there is a beast.'

'Well, what does he know?' Lottie replied. 'We're the

explorers, just like Gam.
She belonged to the
Adventurers' Society, and their
motto was: Be bold, be brave,
be you.'

'That's cool! We should have
our own club,' said Finn.

'Can we keep that motto?'
asked Mia, smiling. 'It suits us!'

'Of course!' cried Lottie.
'We can be the . . . the . . . the
Branksea Adventurers' Club.'

'We should have a special
hand signal just for club

members,' said Mia.

'Great idea!' said Finn,
giving her a high five. 'Hang
on, how about this?'

Finn grabbed Lottie and
Mia's hands and moved them
so they were in a three-way

high five. 'Now let's do three
claps and say the motto,'
he said.

'Be bold, be brave, be you!'
the friends shouted. And so
ended the first meeting of the
Branksea Adventurers' Club.

After school, the Branksea
Adventurers went to Harley
Wood to check their trap.

'Look, there's something
there!' cried Lottie, running to
the tree.

There was a huge print in the mud. It was wide and deep, and at the front it had five dents with sharp claw marks at the ends.

A shiver ran down Lottie's spine. 'That is much bigger than Biscuit's paw print,' she said.

'It's bigger than a cow's hoof!' said Finn.

'It's deep, too,' said Mia. 'The beast must be heavy.'

Lottie sketched a picture of the print in her notebook.

'We have lots of evidence now,' Lottie said.

'I want to see the beast properly!' said Finn.

Mia looked unsure. 'What if it's really, really big?'

Lottie put her notebook and pencil back in her bag. 'Don't forget that we're the Branksea Adventurers!' she said, and gave the others a three-way high five.

On the way home, they passed the Branksea Castle cottages. Lottie noticed that one of the garden walls had been knocked down.

'Gosh,' said Lottie. 'Something big and strong must have knocked that wall over.'

'Just like the fences on my dad's farm,' said Finn.

'And look at this apple crate,' said Mia. 'These claw marks look just like the ones we saw on the tree.'

Suddenly Lottie felt a bit
scared about the beast. It was
strong enough to knock down
walls and hungry enough to eat
an entire crate of apples!

But she shook herself – she was a Branksea Adventurer. She wasn't going to give up her search.

'Should we tell someone about the beast?' asked Mia. 'It seems to be causing a lot of trouble.'

'What about Zara at the Wildlife Centre?' said Finn.

'That's a great idea,' said Lottie. 'Let's meet her at Harley Wood tomorrow and bring all our evidence. She'll know what to do!'

Chapter Six
A Huge Lizard Thing

There was a big crowd in the school's entrance hall when Lottie arrived early the next morning. Sammi was standing on a chair, waving the school newspaper and shouting, 'Read all about the beast of Branksea!'

Lottie was shocked.

Yesterday Sammi had said he didn't believe in the beast!

Mia was standing nearby with her arms crossed. 'Sammi stole my photo and is spreading lies about the beast!' she told Lottie.

Lottie picked up a newspaper. Sammi had written all about a huge, scary beast that was running loose in Harley Wood!

He'd put Mia's photo of the beast's eyes on the front page.

Finn came over. He was holding a copy of the *Branksea School News*, too. 'This says that Sammi saw the beast with his own eyes. That's not true!'

Before the three friends could decide what to do, the bell rang for lessons.

Rumours about the beast grew and grew all day.

'It's bigger than Big Ben,' whispered Amy in assembly.

'Sammi said its claws are like
swords,' said James in Science class.

'Sammi hasn't even seen it!'
Lottie said crossly.

By home time, everyone
wanted to go to the wood to
catch the beast.

'We've got to get there first,' said Lottie. 'Let's tell Zara to meet us there earlier!'

The Branksea Adventurers did their three-way high five, then Lottie went home to fetch Biscuit and ask her mum to call Zara.

Lottie and Biscuit dashed to Harley Wood as soon as they could. Unfortunately, they were not the first ones there.

Zara was standing in front of a big crowd. People were

demanding to know about the
beast of Branksea.

'We have to talk to Zara
alone, without all these people,'
said Mia.

'I have a plan,' said Finn, and
he jumped on to a log.

'Hey, everybody!' he shouted. 'I just saw the beast! It's a huge lizard thing and it's heading for the beach!'

The crowd set off straight away to look for the beast.

Now the friends were free to talk to Zara alone.

Zara sighed and ran her fingers through her cropped hair. 'What do you three know about this beast, then?' she asked.

'It's not really a lizard thing,'

said Lottie. 'But it is real! We found its claw marks, fur and a big print in the mud.'

'And Mia took a photo of it,' said Finn.

Mia showed Zara their evidence.

Zara smiled. 'I'm impressed!' she said. 'What do you think it is?'

'We're not sure,' said Lottie. 'That's why we wanted to see you.'

'Well, I was going to try to see it tonight. If you get your parents' permission, you can join me on a stake-out in the wood,' said Zara. 'That means we sit and wait quietly, and hope the beast comes by!'

Lottie, Mia and Finn looked at each other and grinned. That sounded like exactly the sort of thing that the Branksea Adventurers' Club should do!

Chapter Seven
The Beasts of Branksea

'I've never been on a stake-out before,' said Lottie.

'Me neither,' said Finn.

'I'm excited,' said Mia. 'This is the first real adventure of the Branksea Adventurers' Club!'

Gam's notebook was filled with stake-outs. Lottie had read all about the supplies Gam used to take when beast-hunting, so all three of them had packed bags of their own. When Zara came to collect them, she smiled at how well prepared they were.

'Now, what's the first thing we should do on a stake-out?' Zara said, as they arrived at Harley Wood.

'Find shelter!'

'Build a fire!'

'Find firewood!'

The three friends had lots

of ideas. Zara laughed as they talked over each other.

'You're all right,' Zara said. 'How about we make a shelter first, before it gets too dark?'

They all went off to find
fallen branches in the wood.
Then Zara helped them to build
a frame using the branches.
'We'll fill the gaps with twigs

and leaves,' she said. 'That means we'll keep dry if it rains. This is called a bivouac.'

They put down a waterproof sheet and then left their bags in the bivouac. Zara helped them build a fire. They sat around it, toasting marshmallows and drinking hot chocolate.

'These are delicious!' said Lottie through a mouthful of melted marshmallow.

'All good stake-outs start with a tasty snack,' said Zara.

'Once it gets a bit darker, we
can go and look for the beast.'

Lottie, Mia and Finn glanced
at each other. What if the beast
really was huge and scary?

When they had finished eating
their marshmallows, they set off.

The sun had set and the wood was a little spooky in the darkness.

'Here we are,' said Zara, pointing to a spot behind a large bush. 'Now we just have to wait here quietly for the beast.'

They didn't have to wait long.

Soon they heard a rustling and a snuffling from the next bush.

And out came . . .

'Badgers!' whispered Lottie.

'That's right,' said Zara.
'They used to live on Branksea,
but died out. So the Wildlife
Centre brought a new badger
family to settle here. They're very
shy and we didn't want them to
be disturbed, so we did it in secret.'

'Oh! But what about the giant print we saw?' asked Lottie.

Zara took another look at the drawing of the footprint. 'Well,' she said, 'the toes look like badgers' claws, but it looks like another animal stood in the paw print and made it bigger.'

'So there's no beast of Branksea?' asked Finn.

'There's a whole family of them!' said Mia, pointing to the badgers.

'Are you disappointed, Finn?' Zara asked.

'Not really,' he said. 'It's more exciting to have real, live badgers back in Harley Wood!'

'I'm worried that all this beast nonsense will scare them away again,' said Zara.

'We'll sort that,' said Lottie. She had just had an idea.

Chapter Eight
Wildlife Warden Helpers

At home the next day, Lottie got out all her crafting supplies and invited Mia and Finn over.

'We've got to warn people to stay away from the badgers,' said Lottie.

'But everyone is still hunting for a beast!' said Mia.

'That's why we're going to invite everyone back to the beach to explain,' Lottie replied. 'And we're going to make a sign to keep the badgers safe.'

The friends set to work.

Mia made posters and flyers saying:

The Beast of Branksea revealed! Picnic at Branksea Beach, tomorrow, midday.

Finn helped Lottie to make bunting. They cut out colourful triangles of cloth and wrote on them 'BADGERS LIVE HERE. PLEASE KEEP OUT.'

Lottie couldn't believe how many people turned up for the beach picnic. Everyone was very interested in the beast!

At midday, Zara got up on a log to address the crowd. 'Welcome, everyone!' she said. 'I'm here today to reveal that

the beast of Branksea . . .
doesn't exist!'

The crowd murmured.
Everyone looked confused.

'What knocked down my
fence, then?' asked Finn's dad.

'Badgers!' Zara replied.

The crowd gasped.

'But I thought badgers were extinct on Branksea,' said Lottie's mum.

Zara nodded. 'They were, but the Wildlife Centre just brought them back. I am so sorry if they have disturbed you!'

The picnickers chattered loudly. Some people were disappointed that there wasn't a legendary beast on the island after all. But everyone agreed it was exciting to have badgers back in Harley Wood again.

Zara clapped her hands to shush the crowd.

'I also have to thank three very special people for organizing this picnic, and for creating banners to keep the badgers safe,' she said. 'Lottie, Mia and Finn, I am making you official wildlife warden helpers for all your hard work!'

Everyone cheered as Zara handed each of the three friends a special badge.

Lottie proudly pinned her badge on to her T-shirt. It would have been amazing

to find a beast on the island,
but keeping the badgers safe
was much more important.

That evening, Lottie went and
found the journal she had been
given for Christmas.

'I've been saving this for something special,' Lottie told Biscuit.

She got out her favourite glittery green pen and wrote on the first page 'My Adventure Journal'.

'I'm going to keep a record of all our adventures, just like Gam,' Lottie said.

Biscuit barked and wagged his tail.

Lottie laughed and gave him a hug. 'You may not be able to stand on two legs like a